The Little World

Written and Illustrated by

Cooper Edens

Cooper Co ♥
2007

Blue Lantern Books
1994

ISBN 1-883211-01-8

Blue Lantern Books
PO Box 4399
Seattle, Washington 98104

The Little World
is dedicated to
Polly Klaas.   C.E.

Between you and the sky
something has appeared.
Can you guess what it is?
That is right.
You have discovered
The Little World.

Why are you singing?
Is it because you know
The Little World
will soon join in?

The Little World

is peaceful.
This must be why
you are staring into it
so deeply.

Now...
as it nestles down
in the grass beside you,
take a good look at it.
See with your heart,
if you can place
The Little World.

You recognize
The Little World;
its trees,
its rivers
and its sky.
But, can you remember
from where or when?

Perhaps you,
yourself,
once called
The Little World
your home?

Today...
you can easily put
The Little World
in your pocket.
You can lose it.
So be careful
with **The Little World**,
because,
if you break
The Little World
it will disappear
forever.

What are you doing?
For goodness sake,
don't let
The Little World
out the garden gate!

Let's see if you can find
The Little World now?
You have a long time,
but don't let it get too far
out of your sight.

If you can stay close
to The Little World
it will become you,
and you will become it,
and life will be
what you dream.

In your life...
may you always know
The Little World.
At the end of all your adventures
may you arrive where you started
and know the joy
of **The Little World**
for the first time.

Have fun with
The Little World...
and for your happiness
The Little World
will always return.

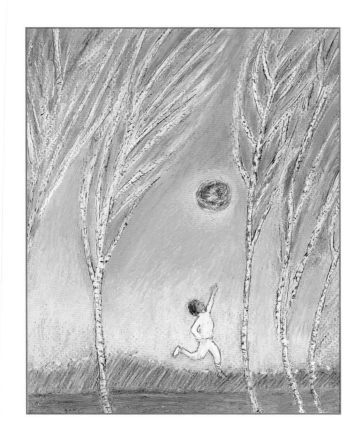

Everytime...
The Little World
returns to you
it will have grown
from the love and care
it has been given.

Someday...
we will live
on the beautiful surface
and breathe the fresh air
of **The Little World.**

The illustrations were created using Caran D'ache crayons on stone blue
cresent board. This book was set in Florentine at the Blue Lantern Studio.